to Alan, with love

Copyright © 1990 Ruth Gembicki Bragg
Published by Picture Book Studio, Saxonville, MA.
Distributed in Canada by Vanwell Publishing, St. Catharines, Ont.
All rights reserved.
Printed in Hong Kong.
10 9 8 7 6 5 4 3 2 1

Library of Congress Cataloging in Publication Data
Bragg, Ruth Gembicki.
Mrs. Muggle's sparkle / Ruth Gembicki Bragg.
Summary: Mrs. Muggle searches for her lost pet bird whom she trained to say "I love you."
ISBN 0-88708-106-1
[1. Birds—Fiction. 2. Lost and found possessions—Fiction.] I. Title.
P27.B7335Mr 1989
[E] —dc19   89-31371

Ruth Gembicki Bragg

Mrs. Muggle's Sparkle

Picture Book Studio

One day Mrs. Maisy Muggle
was busy cleaning Sparkle's
cage when suddenly …

Sparkle flew out of the cage, out of the window and away, away, into the wide and wonderful green, green world.

"Oh no!" Mrs. Muggle moaned. Sparkle was very beautiful. His head was blue, his tail was green, and in between was every color of the rainbow.

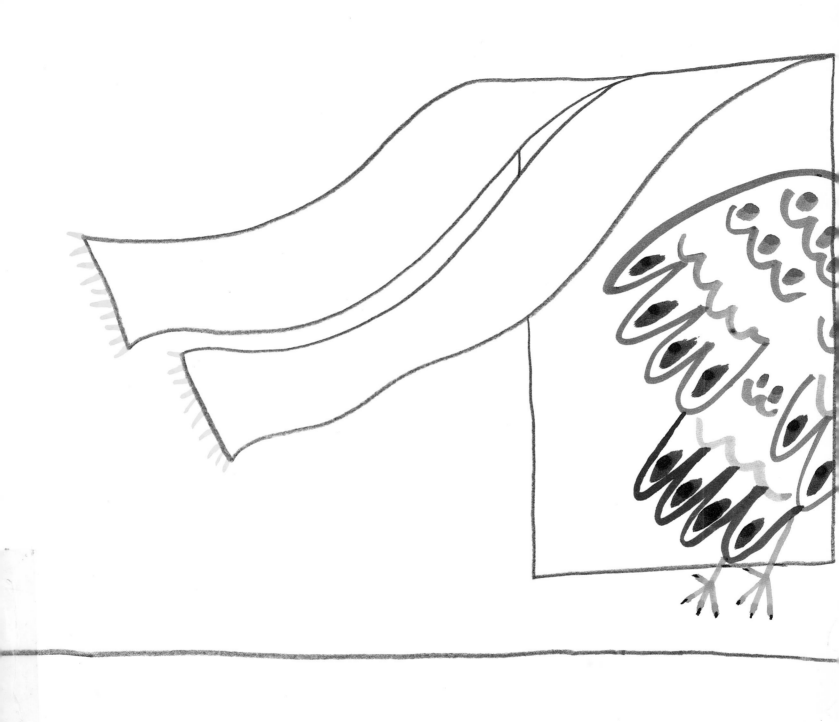

Not only that,
but Mr. Mike Muggle
himself had trained Sparkle
to sit on Maisy's shoulder
and murmur gently
into her ear,

"I love you, I love you."

Now Sparkle was gone.

"I must not panic," Maisy Muggle muttered as she went looking for the beautiful bird that could say such wonderful words.

She looked up in the blue sky. "I love you," she cried. No Sparkle.

She looked up into the green trees. "I love you!" she yelled. No Sparkle.

She looked among the rainbow colored flowers.

"I love you!" she shouted,

AS LOUD AS SHE COULD!

Still no Sparkle.

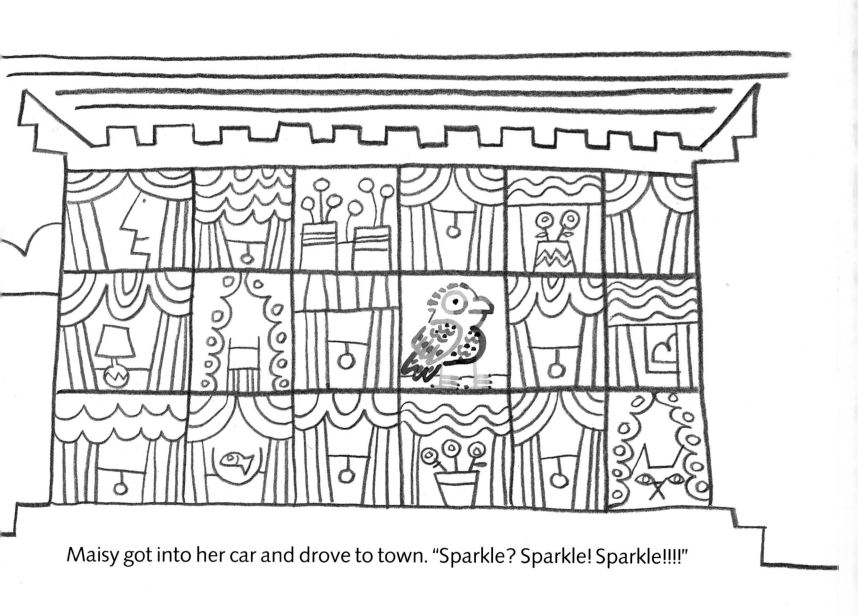

Maisy got into her car and drove to town. "Sparkle? Sparkle! Sparkle!!!!"

Then, there in the window of the Five and Ten was not one Sparkle;

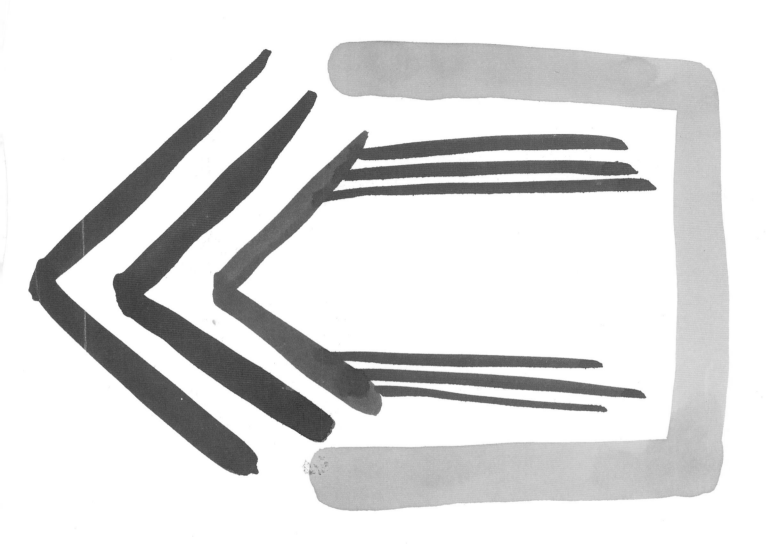

not five Sparkles; but ten, twenty, thirty Sparkles. Maybe even more.

But Mrs. Maisy Muggle's Sparkle, the real Sparkle, the Sparkle with the blue head, the green tail and all the colors of the rainbow in between, the Sparkle that knew how to say "I love you. I love you," because Mike had taught him how, *that* Sparkle was sitting next to another bird with a green head and a blue tail and every color of the rainbow in between, and the real Sparkle was whispering

"I love you.
I love you."

Happily, Maisy took them both home.

Soon the two birds built a nest,

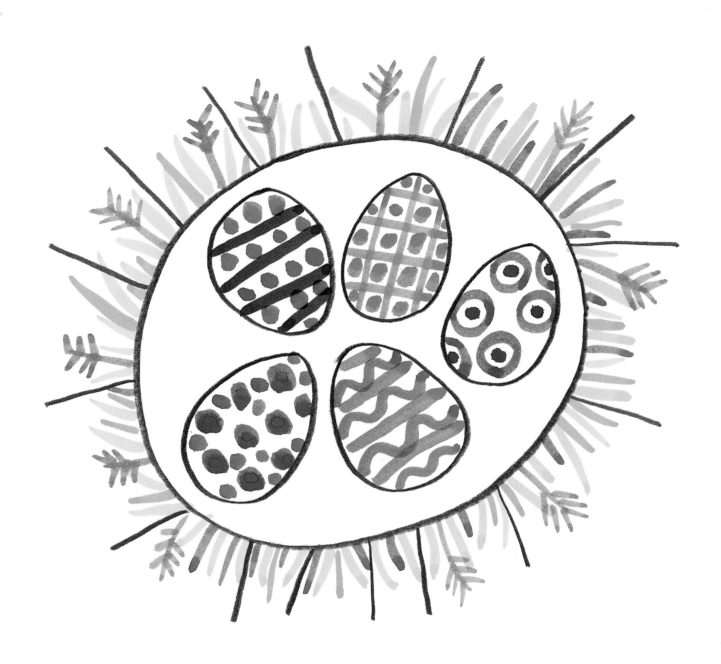

and soon after that there were five eggs,

and as soon as the baby birds could talk, the first words they said were...

and soon after THAT there were five baby birds,

"I'm hungry!"